I Am Known as a Good Girl

"Good as in boring," my brother Philip says. I have three brothers—born bad—who can get away with average report cards. Who have tried cigarettes, steal street signs, and lie to my parents straight-faced. If I ever lied, my parents would crumple to the floor like paper dolls. If I ever talked back, my father would have a heart attack.

There's nothing I can do but dream about being bad.

The Bad Dreams of a Good Girl

The Bad Dreams of a Good Girl

❧ by Susan Shreve ❧

Illustrated by Diane de Groat

BULLSEYE BOOKS · ALFRED A. KNOPF
New York

DR. M. JERRY WEISS, Distinguished Service Professor of Communications at Jersey City State College, is the educational consultant for Bullseye Books. A past chair of the International Reading Association President's Advisory Committee on Intellectual Freedom, he travels frequently to give workshops on the use of trade books in schools.

Library of Congress Catalog Card Number: 81-8359
ISBN: 0-394-83199-3
RL: 5.8

First Bullseye edition: May 1990
Manufactured in the United States of America
10 9 8 7 6 5 4 3 2 1

For Harriet,
who knows children better than anyone,
and for Christy Halvorson

Contents

I. The I Hate Lotty Club

I am known as a good girl.

"Good as in God, at least in this family," my brother Nicholas said when my fourth-grade report card arrived and my father taped it on the refrigerator. None of my brothers, whose report cards are not taped to the refrigerator, could possibly have missed it.

"Good as in boring," my brother Philip said when my father complimented me for keeping my room clean enough so people can walk from the door to the closet to the bed without falling over and dying of head injuries. *Boring* is the only word Philip has used since he turned thirteen. It refers to everyone in the family except him—speaking of people with head injuries.

"Thank goodness for Lotty," my mother said to Aunt Sally on the telephone shortly after Sammy, my oldest brother, ran into Mr. Zoro's Mercedes, which was stopped at a stop sign. Sammy, who had just gotten his license, said he had been concentrating on the stop sign and not on Mr. Zoro's Mercedes.

"If it weren't for Lotty," my mother said in her full-of-tears voice, which she saves for crises, "I could never survive these boys' teenage years."

So there you have it. I have three brothers—born bad—who can get away with average report cards with D's in math. Who have tried cigarettes—even Philip. I saw him. Who steal street signs—a bright green MERCER STREET sign hangs in Nicholas's room, a cheap gift from Sammy on Nicho's twelfth birthday. Who lie to my parents straight-faced. Every Saturday, Sammy packs his book bag and says he's off to the library (which is located in Cassie Starr's basement) to study math, which, according to Nicho, he does between kisses. And my parents never think to ask why he gets D's in trigonometry if he studies in the library every Saturday.

The thing is, my parents love them—even my mother, who has to call my father's office once a day at least to tell him in her crisis voice about the terrible trouble that Nicholas or Sammy or Philip has just gotten into.

I have had no choice. I am the fourth child, and a girl to boot. I had to take what was left and say thank you. I promise you, given half a chance, I would not have chosen to be good.

Think of the responsibility. If I ever lied, my parents would crumple to the floor like paper dolls. If I got a D in anything, even sports, my mother would go to bed, pull the covers up to her chin, and take the telephone off the hook. If I talked back, my father would have a heart attack. So thank you very much, brothers, for taking the best pieces of candy in the box before I was even around to fight for them. There's not a thing I can do but dream about being bad.

I have not always dreamed of being bad, but I have had enough bad dreams of the ordinary kind to go around a family of ten. At least once a week, I have the Black Hole dream. In this dream I am being chased through the park across the street from where I live and I fall into a black hole that does not end—or if it does, I never hit the bottom. But several weeks ago, in the middle of my Black Hole dream, I landed feet first on a dirt floor where the devil looking exactly like Kathy Sanders, lit by a high-beam flashlight, sat cross-legged, making posters with red and blue and green magic markers and decorated with a border of imperfect daisies for the I Hate Lotty Club.

The I Hate Lotty Club was started at the beginning of fourth grade by Kathy Sanders, of course, who was already president of the fourth grade, captain of the figure-skating club, president of Girl Scout Troop 86, and the fastest runner in lower school, boys included. She started the club the second week of classes at Beech Tree Elementary. Beech Tree is the elementary school for gifted children in our area. The only reason I was willing to leave my perfectly good school one block away and go across town to Beech Tree was that my parents, especially my mother, were wild with joy when I was accepted there. If she had known Benny Diggs, a genius in computer math, speaking of boring, had also been accepted at Beech Tree, she might have worried about my future instead of calling every blood relative in America to tell them of my good fortune. My brothers, I should add truthfully, were not equally pleased with the news.

"I plan to eat in my bedroom if we have one more conversation at dinner about exceptional Lotty," Nicholas said.

"Exceptionally boring Lotty," Philip said.

"Go to your room," my father said.

"That will be a great pleasure," Philip said. He was, as a result, grounded for a week.

So, as you might imagine, I had mixed feelings about going to Beech Tree Elementary. Which in no time at all, after I met up with Kathy Sanders, became perfectly clear feelings of blue-black hatred. In fact, as you will soon see, the only person who would sit with me in the lunchroom was Benny Diggs. We usually had a table all to ourselves. That should give you some idea of my situation.

The first week at Beech Tree was heaven. Kathy Sanders invited me over twice to her Farragut Hills mansion, which has singing toilets and a swimming pool. She gave me a list of girls in fourth grade to beware of, boys to ignore, and told me that it was very likely we were going to be best friends forever. At home that night I practiced making dimples like Kathy's by sucking in my cheeks in front of the mirror on the door.

The second week at Beech Tree, I asked Kathy over to my house to spend the night. I could tell within minutes of her arrival that it was not going to work.

"What is there to do?" she asked, lying face down on my bed as though she would shortly die of boredom.

"What are we going to do now?" she asked later while I scrambled desperately through the cupboards looking for ingredients to make a chocolate cake.

"Don't you have a Ping-Pong table?" she asked. Luckily Mrs. Pearson next door does have a Ping-Pong table and let us use it for one game, which Kathy won.

Kathy decided after dinner that she would not spend the night. She was allergic to our Labrador, Fleetwood, and our yellow-striped cat, Marzipan, she said. She didn't feel comfortable around my mother. I should have known then. A dinosaur who suddenly materialized in our living room would feel comfortable around my mother. She has faults, of course, but making people uncomfortable is not one of them.

"Well?" I asked my mother after Kathy had left in a TR-4 with her older brother driving at about a hundred and ninety miles per hour. "What do you think of her?"

My mother was finishing the dishes and didn't reply.

"Tell Lotty what you think, Mama," Philip said.

"She thinks Kathy the creep is trouble," Nicholas said. And she was right.

The I Hate Lotty Club started the following week, but I didn't realize at first that it was a regular organization with dues and rules and club officers with responsibilities. What I did realize was that at gym I was the last chosen for a dodge ball team. For social studies projects no one signed up for Pueblos, which was my Indian tribe. And in music I didn't have a partner for square dancing. All week it was like that. On Friday of the third week I walked into the girls' room and Kathy Sanders was there checking out her Pepsodent smile in the mirror over the sinks.

"I thought we were friends," I finally said to her, full of confusion. I cannot imagine now that I was so stupid.

"You thought wrong," she said, flashing a look for killing witches.

I did not tell my mother at the time. I would handle this problem myself, I decided.

The fourth week of school the girls in the fourth grade gathered in whispering groups when I walked into a room. In language arts I could feel them looking at me strangely as though my face were bruising purple before their eyes. I began to avoid the mirrors when I went to the girls' room afraid that I might see in the mirror that they were right. I could not eat lunch and felt dizzy on the Metro bus going home.

"There's a new club," Benny Diggs said to me one day at lunch. "I guess you know about it." And he very kindly offered me a chocolate-chip cookie, which I took but could not eat.

"I don't," I said. "I hate Beech Tree. I wish I were dumb and didn't have to go here."

Benny Diggs shrugged. As far as he was concerned, I didn't need to wish to be dumb. I already was.

"It's called the I Hate Lotty Club. They asked me to join," he said.

"Who?" I asked, trying to sound as if I didn't really care.

"Kathy Sanders," he said, peeling his orange in

careful sections. "It costs seventy-five cents to join and fifty cents a month afterward."

"For what?"

Benny Diggs shook his head. "They didn't say. All clubs cost money to join, you know. I declined."

I left school that very minute. I excused myself, thanked Benny for the chocolate-chip cookie, went to the locker, got my coat, took the L4 bus to Mercer Street, where I met my mother just as she was getting in the car to look for me.

"They called from the school," she said, hugging me. "I was so worried."

"I left after lunch and I will never go back," I said.

"Lotty," my mother said with the beginnings of her crisis voice.

And I told her everything.

That night my brother Philip took me to see the play *Anne Frank* at his school and afterward we got pizzas at Piago's. He held my hand crossing Elm Avenue even though I cross Elm every day alone when I get off the L4.

The next day Mama called Beech Tree and told them I was sick and we went ice skating at the Galleria.

"What if someone from school sees me and knows I'm not sick?" I asked her.

"Who cares?" she said, and we glided together around the ice like swans.

"You will have to go back to Beech Tree," my father said to me at supper that night.

"Nope," I said.

"If you don't go back, you're letting Kathy Whatever get away with her scheme."

"No," I said.

"Kathy's jealous," Nicholas said thoughtfully. "She's afraid you'll take her place at Beech Tree. You're smart and pretty and athletic," he said.

Well, I almost collapsed. Nicho has not had one decent thing to say about me since I was five and broke my leg falling out of a pecan tree.

That night Sammy came into my room after the light was out, sat down on my bed, and put his hand on my cheek exactly as though he were my father.

"Ignore Kathy Sanders, Lotty," he said. "Pretend she doesn't matter at all."

"Think of it, Carlotta," my father said when he came up to kiss me good night. "You must be an extraordinary child to have a private club named after you."

That night I had a dream about Kathy Sanders. It was Field Day at Beech Tree and we were running in the first heat of the hundred-yard dash. Kathy, of course, was favored to win. In fact, no one at Beech Tree knew I could run, including me. But halfway through the race, some unexpected magic took over and I flew just ahead of Kathy, easily. I could feel her panic. She reached out and grabbed my shorts, looping her fingers in the elastic so she could sail behind me like a kite. In the final sprint to the finish, the elastic on my shorts broke. I grabbed my pants so they wouldn't fall down and leapt across the finish line in first place. Kathy was snapped into the air when the elastic broke, and she landed in the middle of a crowd that was shouting, "Cheater, cheater, cheater."

The next morning I woke up feeling happy.

By the sixth week of school, the I Hate Lotty Club was in full swing.

"I estimate that there is a two-thirds membership in the fourth grade," Benny Diggs told me at lunch, pleased to be able to give me his exact calculations.

"What do they do?" I asked, not really wanting to know.

"It's a secret club," Benny said. "You have to join to find out."

Things were not going well in my classes either. I had failed to hand in two homework papers in math, missed half the questions on the Indian test in social studies, and had fallen asleep on my desk in language arts. In fact, at that very moment, eating lunch with Benny Diggs, I had a private letter to my parents from the fourth-grade homeroom teacher, which I had promised not to read. Of course I read it as soon as the recess bell rang.

Dear Mr. and Mrs. McDaniel,
 We are disappointed in Carlotta's attitude at Beech Tree. She is failing to fulfill the academic requirements and seems unwilling to participate in classroom activities. We should arrange for a conference immediately.

Sincerely,
Adele Hoskinson

So now I was a failure academically as well as socially. Next to me, my brothers were beginning to look like model children.

On my way home from school, I tore up the note from Mrs. Hoskinson and dropped it in the gutter.

At the end of the week, Mrs. Hoskinson asked me why my mother hadn't called her.

"How should I know?" I said, knocked out by my own boldness. "I'm not in charge of her."

Mrs. Hoskinson arranged for me to spend the rest of the afternoon in a chair outside the principal's office.

"Perhaps you would prefer to be back at your old school," the principal said to me at the end of the day.

"I would prefer it very much," I said.

"Your parents will be disappointed," the principal said darkly.

Sammy found me in a low-branched dogwood tree at the park across from our house at dusk.

"Mama's called the police, Lotty," he said, standing at the bottom of the tree.

"Good," I said. "Terrific. I'd love to go to jail."

"She's worried, nitwit. You never came home from school."

"Why should I hurry home? To tell her that I'm flunking everything and going to be kicked out of Beech Tree? I thought she'd rather wait a year or two to see me again."

Sammy carried me home on his shoulders.

"I know about everything," Mama said when I got home.

I didn't let her hug me and she didn't push it.

"I suppose Mrs. Hoskinson called, and the principal, too."

She nodded.

"I tore the note up. You can tell them that," I said.

On the way up to my room, I asked Mama if she'd told the principal about the I Hate Lotty Club.

"No," she said. "I didn't want to say anything about it without asking you first."

"Thank you, Mama," I said, and I meant it.

I wasn't asleep when my brothers came in, but my mind was turned off so it felt like sleep.

Nicholas had an idea.

"Why don't you join the club, Lotty? On Monday, take seventy-five cents to school and join the I Hate Lotty Club."

"What do you mean?" I asked, sitting up in bed.

"Just that," and he gave me the seventy-five cents to join plus fifty cents for the first month's dues.

Sammy wrote the letter, and I copied it over on my mother's best stationery.

> Dear Kathy,
>
> I understand that a new club has formed in fourth grade of which you are the president. I also understand that you are trying to get full membership of the class and I don't want to keep you from reaching your goal. Enclosed is seventy-five cents to join and fifty cents for the first month's membership.
>
> Sincerely,
> Lotty McDaniel

I took the note to school and taped it on Kathy Sanders's locker.

"I'll bring your name up at the next meeting," she

said, looking straight past me after homeroom.

The next meeting was held that day at recess. When I went to the playground, almost everyone in the class was sitting in a circle behind the swings and Kathy Sanders was talking to them. I climbed on the jungle gym and lay on my stomach trying to appear unconcerned. I couldn't hear what was being said, but the meeting was short. I rested my chin on the bar and watched Kathy with some of her slaves saunter over.

"You're voted in," she said as she walked past me.

"So what do I do now?" I asked.

"Nothing," she said. "I'll let you know when there's another meeting."

At lunch in the middle of the week, Benny Diggs said he had bad news for me. The I Hate Lotty membership had dropped off by twenty percent. Kathy Sanders had resigned as president because there were too many demands on her time. There didn't seem to be enough interest in the cause among the other members to keep the club going.

"Children get easily bored," Benny said matter-of-factly, as though it had been years since he had been a child himself.

On Friday Kathy Sanders asked me if I'd like to go ice skating at the Galleria. I said no, thank you very much, I could not. I had been invited to go to the movies with another friend. Which wasn't true. The next morning Kathy called and, without a word of prompting from me, Nicholas said that I had gone ice skating with a friend who had, he added with great pleasure, a rink in her own backyard.

"Kathy Sanders is desperate to have you over," Nicho said, and he picked me up, threw me over the back of the couch, and tickled my stomach until I screamed.

That night when my mother tucked me in, she said Mrs. Hoskinson had called about my attitude.

"What did you tell her?" I asked, expecting the worst.

"I said I wasn't worried about your attitude. Everyone gets D's from time to time."

"I thought you'd collapse if I ever got a D," I said.

"And now you know I won't," she said, leaning down and kissing me on my forehead. "Sweet dreams."

II. The Story of a Short-Term Orphan

I have always been interested in orphans. When I was quite small, I imagined that I was an orphan my parents had picked up in a Houston police station when they went in to register their bikes. My mother had ridden me home in the wicker basket on her handlebars.

"Absolutely true," Nicholas said when I asked him whether he had heard that story.

"No, Carlotta," my mother said in her I-don't-have-time-for-this-conversation voice when I asked her.

"You've got your facts confused, Lotty," Sammy told me. "You were an orphan, of course, but the electrician brought you when he came to fix the dryer. He asked Mama would she like to have you, and she said, 'Why not?' and the electrician replied, 'You'll find out why not soon enough,' and he rolled his eyes."

For a moment I believed Sammy.

"Gospel truth," Sammy sang. "Cross my heart and hope to die. Boy Scouts' honor."

And so I dropped my orphan story for a while.

Recently I've been thinking about orphans again. I'd like to have a large house in the country with plenty of animals and take in orphans. I'd run a school in which we'd study snakes and raccoons and learn to read by making movies of stories we'd write ourselves. I'd forget about mathematics. Once a year, I'd travel around the world collecting orphans. I don't plan to be married or have children of my own. Which should not surprise you. Anyone my age with three older brothers would be crazy to think about marriage. I imagine with thirty or forty orphans, I'll be happy enough.

I never thought that I wanted absolutely to be an orphan until two days ago, Monday, January 19th, to be exact, when I came home from school.

Things had been going better at Beech Tree since the I Hate Lotty Club folded for lack of funds in late October. My grades were not brilliant, but they were acceptable. I was making friends, although I should say, if you don't know this already, that girls in fourth grade can change their minds about a friendship—that is, go from love to hate—in a matter of seconds. So I was never sure whether I was going to have the same friends at the end of language arts class as I had at the beginning. It can make you a little nervous.

However, this Monday was a flat-out, low day in my history of Mondays. First period I mixed up the directions in math and forgot to invert and multiply the division problems in fractions. This gave Mr. Ace-in-the-hole-Grant a golden opportunity to use me as an example of a careless student's failure to follow directions. He spent a whole thirty minutes on my stupidity.

By the time class was over, I had lost two friends, Betsy Overs and Franny Cox. Franny particularly is the kind of girl who will stop her friendship with you on a dime if you forget to invert and multiply.

Then gym was canceled because it was raining, and we had macaroni for lunch.

All of these disappointments in what could have been a perfectly decent day did not matter as much as what happened at three-thirty when I took my house key out of my book bag and let myself in the front door.

The house was completely empty. It still smelled of eggs from breakfast. The dishes were piled in the sink. The newspaper was stacked by the chair in the living room where my father always reads it before he takes the bus to work. The house was cold and damp, and my mother had been in such a hurry to leave that she had not even written me a note to welcome me home on my first day as the orphan child of working parents.

I knew, of course, that my mother was beginning the first job she'd had since Nicholas was born. We had toasted her success Sunday night at supper. I drank half a glass of white wine and fell asleep on the couch. I knew the house would be empty when I came home until five o'clock when Nicho and Philip got back from soccer practice. I had been given a long list of instructions on what to do if and what not to do if not, plus my mother's telephone number at her new job as an assistant editor for *Chance* magazine. It is, however, one thing to know these things in your brain and another to have them happen to you.

The wonderful house where I had grown up was as dark and empty as a coffin.

I went into the kitchen and took down the instructions tacked to the bulletin board. At the bottom was my mother's telephone number. I dialed.

"Good afternoon—*Chance*," the woman at the other end of the phone said.

"Is Mrs. McDaniel there?" I asked.

"Mrs. McDaniel?" There was a pause.

For a moment, I panicked. Mama wasn't there. She had made up her job, out of the blue, I decided. She had no intention of going to work. She had left.

Bolted. Cindy Aldrich's mother had done that just before Christmas. "Too much," she had shouted one afternoon after coming home loaded down with Christmas packages. "It's just too much," she'd said, according to Cindy. "Too many children. Too many dishes and dirty clothes and fingerprinted walls and problems." And by dinner time she had emptied her closet and was off to who knows where. Certainly Mr. Aldrich, who never wanted children in the first place, didn't know where. Or Cindy and her brothers who just wanted a Siamese cat.

"Oh, yes," the woman at the other end of the phone said. "Mrs. McDaniel just started today."

Then she made me hold on for half an hour.

"She's in a planning meeting," the woman said when she finally came back on the wire. "Can I have her return your call?"

"No," I said. "This is her daughter. It's an emergency," I added without a second's thought.

"Lotty?" my mother's voice came on very soon. "What's the matter?"

"I'm sick," I said. She should have been able to tell without asking, just by listening to my voice.

"How? Headache?"

"Yes," I said.

"Do you know what your temperature is?" she asked.

"I think it's high," I said.

I was feeling terrible. Not hot, but terrible.

"You go upstairs, get the thermometer out of the medicine cabinet, leave it in for three minutes, and I'll call you back."

I did not bother. I knew the answer. My skin was exactly the temperature of iced tea.

I answered the telephone before it stopped ringing the first ring.

"It's not so high," I said.

"Then get some juice, crawl into bed with a good book, and I'll be home at six, darling."

"Darling," I thought. She calls the cat darling and sometimes Mrs. Dickinson next door.

"Mama," I said.

"You'll be fine, Carlotta," she said emphatically.

"Maybe not," I thought, but I didn't say that.

When Nicholas and Philip came home, I was in

my parents' bed under the covers. I didn't answer when they called, "Lotty," all around the house, up and down the stairs. I kept my eyes closed.

"For Chrissake, why didn't you answer, Lotty?" Philip said, charging into my mother's bedroom. "Why didn't you answer? I thought something had happened to you."

"It has," I said.

"What?" he asked. He picked up my father's brush and fixed his hair with his back to me—very concerned as you can tell.

"I am really extremely sick," I said weakly.

"Where?"

"All over."

"Did you call Mama?"

"Of course I did. I called her at her new job. It didn't seem to matter a bit to her."

And I closed my eyes, pretending to sleep, and dreamed of being an orphan.

Our lives had started to go bad last summer, before Beech Tree. We didn't have the usual wonderful summer at the cabin miles from town. We rented the cabin, but Daddy said he couldn't come with us.

"For just a week, Douglas?" my mother begged in a voice that comes on her before she loses her temper.

"No," my father said, not pleasantly. "I can't break away at all this summer."

My father is a lawyer. Let me tell you that if I were given the choice of being a lawyer or a prisoner, I would choose prisoner without a second's thought. The life is pretty much the same, I imagine, as that of a lawyer, but prisoners get more sympathy.

"Besides," my father said, "I can't afford it."

"You can't afford not to take a vacation," my mother said. "You're working night and day as it is. A lot of good you'll be to your clients in a hospital with a heart attack."

"Don't be extreme," my father said, giving my mother a killing look across the dinner table.

I knew the direction the conversation was going to go in, and I would have left the dinner table immediately if I had been allowed.

"Then I suppose we'll all stay home this summer," my mother said in the voice my brother

Sammy calls her nailed-on-the-cross voice.

"It's up to you," my father said. "I know what I have to do." And then he slammed his hand on the kitchen table, which he does when he wants us to listen to him, as though we don't listen to him in the first place. "You could always go back to work yourself, Maggie."

I expected my mother to laugh and say, "Don't be silly, Douglas," or to lose her temper and say, "Not until Lotty is in high school," but she didn't say either.

Instead, she said in a surprisingly pleasant voice, "Of course, I could do that."

"Most mothers work today," Nicholas said to me when I told him the bad news. "You're lucky you've had Mama at home this long to baby you."

"We need the money," Sammy said earnestly, as though he'd just turned forty-two with gray hair. "It costs a fortune to live today."

"Jeez, Lotty, you are nine, you know. Do you expect Mama to shrivel up in the house waiting until you get married?"

It wasn't as if she stayed in the house doing

laundry all day. She taught ballet and organized the art program for the elementary school and worked at the museum and did free-lance editing for a magazine. But, as Nicholas pointed out to me with no sympathy, she was at home when I came home and so, as far as I was concerned, she didn't have any other life but us.

"This is difficult for Lotty," Mother said when she overheard our conversation. "Don't make it harder."

"It's time Lotty grew up," Nicholas said.

"As if you're grown up," I snapped.

"In the brain, dummy. I'm grown up in the brain," he said.

"Like a teenage ape," I said.

But there was a lot of truth to what Nicholas said, and I was worried all fall about what would happen to me when my mother went to work. Even before she found a job, she began to change. She cut her hair and wore stockings and high heels. She went on a diet and bought new clothes. Often she had other things on her mind. I had to tell her several times when I came home from school what had happened that day, and then she'd smile, deaf as a doornail, and say, "That's very nice, Lotty."

"You didn't even hear what I said," I'd tell her, but she didn't even defend herself.

It took her all fall to find a job, and I began to have false hopes. She'd been a mother too long. No one would want an old editor who hadn't worked for twelve years. She couldn't adjust.

"Well?" my father would ask carefully at supper on a day my mother was expecting to hear about one job or another. She must have tried for a hundred and fifty at least.

"Nope," she'd say sadly, and my heart would leap for joy.

"It'll take time," my father said. "You'll find something soon, Maggie."

I doubted it. In fact, as the autumn went by and the days got shorter and shorter toward Christmas, I was certain that Mother would give up looking. I even felt sorry for her because she had certainly tried hard. Perhaps, I began to hope, she would be offered a job and turn it down because with a job she wouldn't have time for Christmas preparations.

So I was unprepared for the bad news that came on December 1st, just in time to ruin Christmas.

"Mama's been hired as an editor for *Chance*," Nicho said to me when I came home from my piano lessons.

"Terrific," I said. "Terrific, Mama," I called to her. I am not a good enough actress to have risked congratulating her face-to-face, so I ran upstairs, closed the door to my bedroom, and cried my eyes out.

Mother did not come upstairs for a long time. When she finally did, I heard her in her own room first and then on the telephone and much later she came into my room and sat down beside me on the bed.

"What's the trouble, angel," she asked, not even suspecting the truth after nine years as my mother.

"Kathy Sanders again," I lied.

She patted me on the back. "Kathy's not worth thinking about," she said absently.

It crossed my mind that I could say the I Hate Lotty Club was back in business or that I was flunking language arts to keep Mother from going to work at *Chance*.

But, of course, as you already know, nothing happened to stop her.

When Mother came home from work after her first day, I felt immediately better. But I didn't get up. I certainly didn't want anyone to know that it was her not being there making me sick and not my body.

My body in fact was perfectly fine, as Mama pointed out to me at supper when I suggested that I stay home on Tuesday.

"What will happen now that you're working if I get extremely sick at school?" I asked my mother later that night.

"We'll face that when it happens," she said.

I shrugged. That is not my idea of safety—facing things when they happen.

"Mama thinks you may have gotten sick because she's gone to work," Nicholas said with his usual sensitivity before he went to bed that night.

I threw my sneaker straight at him, but he caught it and without a word put it down on my bed.

The next morning I was honest-to-God sick—a sore throat and temperature, miracle of miracles.

"Damn," my mother said when she read the thermometer. She tucked me into bed, sent Nicho for juice, and finished dressing.

When she came back to my room in a dress and high heels with peach-colored cheeks and blackened eyelashes, I knew for a fact that I could have a terrible case of ringworm and she would go to work.

"Daddy's going to take you to the doctor," she said to me.

"Fine," I said, not looking at her directly. "I suppose you are going to work," I said in my I-couldn't-care-less voice.

"I am. If the doctor is concerned, I'll come home, Lotty. If not, Daddy will make sure you have plenty of juices and aspirin before he goes to work and I'll call to check on you every couple of hours."

"You mean I'll be home alone?"

"You'll be fine," she said.

"Perfectly," I said in a chilly voice. I certainly was not going to let her know, since it hadn't occurred to her, that by three o'clock I could die of severe strep throat or choke on an aspirin.

I could have predicted that my father wouldn't be able to find the doctor's office. He had never taken us there. We were half an hour late.

"I'm sorry to be so much trouble," I said, not really meaning it.

"Don't be silly, Lotty," he said.

Dr. Groover said there was no problem—I had a virus and should be back in school in a couple of days. When my father asked about leaving me alone all day, the doctor said it was a great idea, good for developing independence. It's too bad Dr. Groover never got invited to join the I Hate Lotty Club. He would have made an outstanding member.

It took my father thirteen seconds to get juice, take out the aspirin, tuck me into bed, and leave for his office where very important business was waiting for him.

So there I was alone. Nine thirty in the morning and six hours before another human being would walk into the house. Unless, of course, we had a robber.

"Have you thought of robbers?" I asked my mother when she called at nine forty-seven.

"We haven't had crime in the neighborhood for years," she said. "Besides, Fleetwood is with you."

That was some comfort. If a robber were to come to the door, our dog Fleetwood would open it, jump on the robber's shoulders and lick his ears. And while the robber was clearing out the silver and tying me, gagged, to the bedposts, Fleetwood would climb on the velvet couch in the living room and fall asleep.

It was a measure of my mother's disinterest in me that she believed I'd be safe with Fleetwood.

"I wish I were an orphan," I said. "I am an orphan," I said and slammed down the phone.

In my daydream of orphans, I left home. When my mother came back from work that afternoon, my bed was neatly made and a note decorated with a border of clover read: "See you in Shanghai, Best wishes to you and yours. Carlotta." I'd spend the first night at Benny Diggs's house who wouldn't know the difference. The second day, I'd go to the mayor of Houston's house and offer my services cleaning, taking care of pets, clipping hedges. The mayor is extremely well liked, rich, and important. So is his wife, who greeted me at the door with tears in her eyes.

"I have never had a little girl," she said to me. "Only boys. I would love to have you live with us."

Easy as pie. I didn't even have to comb my hair.

I moved in with the mayor and his wife. I had a beautiful room with daisy wallpaper and a canopy bed. Fortunately all of the mayor's sons are married and live elsewhere. The mayor's wife refused to allow me to do a bit of work. I was sent to private school and given my own telephone. There was talk of a horse for my birthday.

My mother, of course, was very sorry she had treated me so badly.

"Carlotta is a lovely child," the mayor's wife told Mama when she called. "I can't understand why you didn't want her. I have dropped all of my responsibilities as a mayor's wife to be here when Carlotta gets home from school."

My parents felt terrible. They sent my brother Nicholas to the mayor's house, and he begged me to come home. My mother, he said, was miserable without me and couldn't eat. They sent my brother Sammy, and he said that my father was going to sue the mayor's wife for kidnapping. They sent my brother Philip, and he cried so hard when he saw me that the mayor's cleaning lady had to mop the floor.

At that point in my daydream the telephone rang. It was my mother.

"Have you had your juice?" she asked.

"No," I said.

"Then have some," she said, "and look under your pillow."

I went downstairs and got a glass of grape juice. I made toast and jam and read the front page of the newspaper with all the bad news. I fed Marzipan and dragged Fleetwood off the velvet couch where he was sleeping. Then I went back to my room, climbed in my non-canopy bed, and looked under the pillow. There was a note on my mother's best stationery.

> Dear, dear Lotty,
>   This morning I remember very clearly the first time you walked away from me across the living room floor on your own, so full of pleasure because you would not have to be carried any longer. It made me cry because I knew you were my last baby and I wanted to be able to carry you longer.
>   Changes are difficult, whether you are forty-two, like me, or nine. This morning I would like to call my office and stay at home with you. But change is also good once you get used to it. Wouldn't I be in fine shape and you, too, if you had not learned to walk and I still had to carry you—back and forth to school, up and down stairs, over to your friends' house?
>   I love you. M.

At lunchtime, I went downstairs and made a tunafish sandwich with a lot of onion, which Mama never uses, and ate in front of the television soap,

"And So Tomorrow." Even when I'm sick, Mama doesn't let me watch the soaps.

After Gerald was in a plane crash, crippled from the neck down, and Annie got a divorce to marry him, I turned off "And So Tomorrow" and did the breakfast dishes and vacuumed the living room rug. Then I turned the stereo on top volume and made the beds, even my parents'. I looked up a recipe for spaghetti, which I made and burned, of course, and a cake for dessert, which was very thick at one end and very thin at the other. The icing was too thick to spread, but I made a design of chocolate dots all over the top of the cake. It looked quite good, I thought.

Twice my mother called, once to see what my temperature was and I'd forgotten to take it, and once to see if I'd had more juice, which I had. Both times, I didn't mention that I'd found her note and she didn't ask me.

But I was feeling much better. In fact, quite good, except for the sore throat. The house looked cleaner than it had that morning. I even brushed all of Fleetwood's black hair off the sofa. And dinner, a little burned but okay otherwise, was almost ready. At two thirty, I watched a creepy hospital soap opera on television. Then I read a magazine Philip shouldn't have had hidden under his bed, tried on my mother's makeup, and was sitting at the desk in the library doing the homework Benny Diggs had brought me when Nicho and Philip walked into the house.

"You look better," Nicho said.

"Was it lonely?" Philip asked.

"Nope, not really," I said.

"Were you scared?" Nicho asked. "I thought you might be scared."

"With Fleetwood here?" I said, and we all laughed.

When I finished my homework, I cut out a red construction-paper heart the size of an apple and wrote, "I love you, too—Love, Little Orphan Lotty," and put it on my mother's pillow where she couldn't miss it.

III. The Mystery of Fathers

In April, just after Easter vacation, my father tripped over Fleetwood, who was lying on the front porch, and fell down eight steps onto the cement sidewalk. One doctor said he had torn a ligament in his back, another that he had bruised his spine, a third that he had cracked a vertebra. Each one said that bed rest would be necessary. My father disagreed with all of them. He was about to get a fourth opinion when my mother pointed out that even if he saw every one of the twenty-four orthopedic doctors listed in the yellow pages, he would still have to go to bed for a week.

"You're waiting for a doctor who will tell you that you're fine. That you can go back to work."

My father agreed that she was right.

"Well you're not fine," my mother said. "You can hardly move." And she brought him iced tea and fresh strawberries and made him go to bed with a heating pad under his back. She unplugged the telephone next to the bed and took it downstairs.

"I'll probably lose half my clients if I'm out for a week."

"Probably," my mother agreed.

"You're sure there are no pills for this?" he asked. "Why don't you call that last doctor and make certain."

"Bed rest, darling. They all said bed rest."

"It's lucky he's not sick often," Nicho said at Sunday lunch.

"You'd think the world had come to an end," Philip agreed.

My mother laughed.

"Your father has never missed a day of work since we've been married. He *is* afraid the world will come to an end without him."

He complained all of Sunday. The soup, he said, was too cold. And when Mother offered to heat it again, he said he didn't like cream of chicken soup anyway. The room, he said, was too hot. Would someone get a fan in the attic and bring him a blanket just in case the fan gave him a chill? The traffic on the street bothered him, and so did the voice of Mrs. Peachtree next door calling Charlie Peachtree home for lunch. He decided he'd rather live in a house in the country away from the Peachtrees whom he had never liked.

At four o'clock he decided that he wanted the whole family to go out to dinner so he could rest quietly. But then, just as we started to go out the door, he changed his mind and said he didn't want to be left alone.

Monday there was a teachers' meeting at Beech Tree Elementary and school was out. That meant I would be home all day alone with Daddy. I mentioned this trial to Mother at the dinner we ended up eating in the kitchen at home.

"Good luck," Nicho said.

"It should be a fun-packed day," Sammy said.

Philip kindly considered staying home with me since he hadn't done his history and math homework, but when Daddy lost his temper at poor stupid Fleetwood, Philip decided to do his math and history homework and go to school instead.

"Anyway, Lotty," Mother said when she kissed me good night, "it will be a good chance for you and Daddy to get to know each other better."

I should mention that I have never felt absolutely comfortable around my father.

"It's because he's shy and doesn't exactly know what to say to you," my mother once said to me.

Maybe. But he doesn't seem particularly shy to me. He can talk about law all day without an awkward moment. He and Nicho can rattle off baseball scores hour after hour, and he can argue with Sammy about the United States involvement with Communist bloc countries as he does every night at dinner. He just doesn't have anything to say to me.

"Because I'm a girl," I tell my mother. She does not disagree, but she says he will change his mind as I get older.

Lately I've noticed that he is quite handsome, as fathers go. His hair is still black and thick and falls over his forehead when he's excited, like Philip's does. He has almond-shaped eyes that are almost green and a nose so narrow at the bridge that his glasses are always falling halfway down. I like the way he looks when he's thinking. In fact, the other day I was sitting in his study reading a Nancy Drew and watching him at his desk when I had a sudden urge to sit in his lap, which I haven't done for years and years. I didn't, of course. He's not the sort of father who welcomes lap-sitting. Or so I've always thought.

On Monday morning I had breakfast with the rest of the family, who failed as usual to do their own dishes before they left for work and school.

"You might take breakfast up to Daddy," Mother said before she left. It wasn't an order. For a long time I sat in the kitchen surrounded by the breakfast dishes and thought about what I would say to him when I did bring his breakfast. And what he would say to me.

Perhaps, "I hate fried eggs and, besides, these are broken."

Or, "You know I never drink orange juice, Lotty, and the coffee is cold."

Or, nothing at all.

That, I decided, was what worried me. There I was in the house alone with my father, whom I hardly knew. What if we had nothing to say to each other for the next eight hours until Nicholas and Philip got home from school.

To stall for time, I did the dishes, thinking of possible topics of conversation. We could, I supposed, talk about my summer plans, which were to start a newspaper. Or the I Hate Lotty Club, which no longer existed and probably wouldn't interest him anyway. We could talk about his back.

I heard him walking around upstairs. He shouted at Marzipan to get off the bed, and then he called me in the same voice he had used with the cat and I ran upstairs.

He was standing at the bottom of the bed, holding onto the bedpost with one hand and onto his back with the other, bent double like a very old man, an expression of pain on his face.

"Would you mind bringing me a cup of coffee?" he asked. "Hot."

I was afraid to ask if he needed help. I didn't even want to stay in the room. I could tell immediately that he didn't want me to see him that way, so I took Marzipan downstairs with me and decided to surprise him with a real breakfast.

I decided on scrambled eggs because I was sure I'd break the yolks with fried. I toasted English muffins and picked three tulips from the garden to put on his tray in a jelly glass.

I wrote a note, "For Mr. McDaniel from his loving daughter, Carlotta," and drew a small picture of him as a stick figure bent in half with turned-down lips.

When I took the tray upstairs, I found him

propped up with pillows and talking on the telephone, which he had recovered from Philip's room. I put the tray down on his bed and went to my own room to make a costume for the fourth-grade play in which I was going to be a pigeon.

My father is always talking business on the telephone. It can go on for hours on weekends and in the evening after he has presumably come home to be with us. So I was quite surprised when after just a few minutes he called me into his room.

He was sitting on the edge of his bed when I came in. I noticed that he had put the glass of tulips on the table beside the telephone.

"Thank you for the flowers," he said, "and the note."

He handed me a piece of paper folded in fours, which I started to put in my pocket.

"Read it," he said.

"Dear Carlotta," I read to myself. "Already I feel better with the yellow tulips you brought. I'm very glad not to be at work today." At the bottom was a stick figure of a man with a turned-up smile.

I felt suddenly shy and could tell that he did

too—that he was probably wondering what in the world a forty-five-year-old man could say to his nine-year-old daughter.

"What are we going to do today?" he asked.

"I have to make a pigeon costume. I'm going to sew feathers on long underwear and make a pigeon head."

He suggested that I make the costume on his bed—that he needed to work and it would be less lonely for him if we worked together.

In my bedroom, I changed clothes. I tried on my blue jeans with a red heart turtleneck, but I looked too ordinary. I tried on a pair of corduroys with a western shirt, which was better but not quite right. I checked my mother's closet and found just what I wanted—a boys' blue-striped shirt. It was too long at the sleeves, so I rolled them up. Then I brushed my hair loose around my face without barettes. I've never seen my mother in barettes. I checked the mirror on my door and decided to use my mother's rose blush and figured that except for the obvious absence of breasts filling the blue-striped shirt, I

could pass for a sixth- or seventh-grader. I gathered my pigeon costume and went to my parents' bedroom. Marzipan had taken her place on my mother's pillow.

My father looked up from his work and suggested I settle at the bottom of the bed. Which I did, dumping my feathers and sewing box and arranging myself so I could lean against the four-poster directly opposite where my father was working.

I threaded a needle and began stitching real pigeon feathers to the gray long underwear, conscious, I realized, less of my project than of my father at the other end of the bed. In the middle of my sewing the first feather, he threw a piece of paper at me. It was folded and had CARLOTTA printed on top in bold letters. I opened it.

"You look smashing in your mother's shirt," he had written.

I probably blushed. "She doesn't mind if I borrow her clothes," I said. "Are you ready for lunch?" I asked.

"No," he said. "Just company."

By one o'clock when the telephone rang, I had a pile of notes beside me on the bed and the top half of my costume was finished.

It was my mother on the telephone. My father seemed to be very glad to talk to her and they talked forever about absolutely nothing.

"You just saw her two hours ago," I snapped when my father hung up the phone.

I couldn't understand my bad temper.

I went downstairs to make lunch. There was nothing but peanut butter and cheddar cheese, so I went to the deli, two blocks away, and got cold salmon, potato salad, French bread and apple cider.

"My father is sick, so I'm making him a special lunch," I told Frank behind the counter.

"An expensive lunch," he said and agreed to let me pay him half the bill later because I only had five dollars. "Ten dollars for one lunch," he said and shook his head.

On the way home, I picked the Peachtrees' daffodils from their side yard out of view of the house. I had never done that before. I set the tray with Mother's best linen, which she no longer uses because she doesn't have time to iron now that she's working. Next to the daffodils, I put another note. It said, "I hope you like the lunch. It was *very* expensive. Love, Lotty."

He was on the telephone, of course, when I came up. To my astonishment he told the person on the other end of the line that I was there and he would have to hang up. Which almost, not quite, made up for the long conversation he'd had with my mother.

During lunch my father told me that he was thinking about leaving the law firm and setting up an independent practice. He had not really discussed it seriously with my mother, he said, so he asked me to keep it to myself. He told me about the year when he was in fourth grade and his mother died unexpectedly and how lonely he'd been although he had never admitted it to anyone at the time. He told me that in college he had not been asked to join a fraternity because he was too serious and studious. Shortly after lunch, he stacked the papers he had been working on, put them in his briefcase, and zipped it shut. He said he wanted to talk to me for the rest of the afternoon.

I finished my pigeon costume while we talked and even had time to make the head. It wasn't terrific, but it was good enough, considering how far away I would be from the audience. Just before Philip and Nicholas came home, when I heard them storming up the front walk, I wrote my last note: "Dear Daddy," it said. "In spite of what the fraternities thought at college, I think you are handsome and not too serious. Love, Carlotta."

And then Philip was there talking about soccer practice and how he hated to play center, and Nicho was complaining about flunking physical science because the teacher had it in for him, and Mother called again although she was going to be home in an hour. So I left my parents' bedroom with my completed pigeon costume and went to my room where I tried to do my math homework without a bit of success. It occurred to me, listening to the conversations between my father and brothers in the next room, that my father only cared about me when no one else was around. I lay face down on my bed and began a dream in which I took all of the notes my father had written me into his room, dumped them on his bed, and very pleasantly asked to borrow some matches. Which, of course, I used to light the notes and the bed, burning them all instantly to the ground. In the middle of my second go-round on the same dream, Philip called to say there was a delivery man at the front door with something for me and I should go downstairs.

The man at the door was from Friendship Florist, and he was holding a long white package.

"Carlotta McDaniel?" he asked.

I nodded and he gave me a paper to sign to prove I had received the package. Then he gave me the package. I took it and waited until he had gone down the front steps before I opened the white paper. Inside were six long-stemmed red roses with a note: "Thanks for one of the nicest days I've had in years. Love, Daddy."

IV. The Unexpected Danger of Bad Dreams

I have trouble with my brother Philip. Every few months we declare an all-out military war against each other. At its worst, this can last at a high level of danger for almost a week. Neither of us has ever been injured in battle, but recently Philip hung all of my dolls, naked and upside down, by a rope out of the bathroom window. So I wrote I LOVE CASSIE in ruby-red nail polish on the back of his blue jeans. Which was the beginning of my bad dream about the rapid and unfortunate downfall of Philip McDaniel.

According to Mother, who always insists on finding reasons for everything, the trouble between us started years ago when I was just learning to walk. Apparently I discovered that if I quietly pinched Philip on the bottom, he would hit me. Not hard enough to hurt, of course, but hard enough to pretend it hurt.

"Philip hit me," I'd cry.

"She pinched me," he'd tell Mama. And I'd look very surprised and say, "I did not." And Philip would get punished, to my delight. I cannot imagine that I was that kind of a child, but everyone, including my grandmother who can't imagine much, remembers these incidents.

Ever since then, if trouble develops in our family, it's a good bet that it will be between Philip and me. At least that's the way it was until a week ago. Last Monday, however, Philip and I signed a truce, which says among other things that we will not dream bad dreams about each other again, since we know now that they can come true.

Our final war started on a hot day in April after

school. I had come straight home to make a tunafish casserole for dinner so I could go skating at the Galleria with my half-enemy, Kathy Sanders. Since Mother started her new job, she has us all organized with chores detailed on lists in the kitchen.

"As though we're Mama's trained rats," Philip said bitterly when he came in from school to find me burning a white sauce on the stove.

"Yuck," he said looking at the pan of gray-white lumps in different sizes. "I'm going to be sick."

"Great idea," I said, not looking up.

"Tuna and lumps," he said, opening the refrigerator, taking out the milk, and drinking straight from the carton.

"Don't, Philip," I said. "That's disgusting."

"You should be an expert on disgusting," he said, dumping his book bag on the table and settling into his math.

Each of us cooks once a week as part of Mother's new organization. Philip cooks hot dogs and baked beans. Nicholas cooks chicken, which he puts in a bag and shakes and bakes. Sammy cooks spaghetti, and once he made a cheesecake that tasted like a cherry-flavored sponge. I cook something different each week because I get bored easily. Mostly it's bad, but at least it's different.

"There weren't any lumps in the sauce until you came in, you know," I said to Philip.

"Sure," he said, buried in his math. "Little Suzy Snowcrop, Queen of the Kitchen. My apologies."

I was at that very moment opening a large can of Bumblebee tuna and a terrible thought overcame me before I had a chance to be sensible. Philip was bending over his homework, his hair covering his eyes so he could see the page but couldn't see me coming. I tiptoed over, lifted the can of tunafish over his head and tilted it so a thin stream of oil zipped through the air, onto his head, and ran down his bangs to his nose before dripping onto the page of neatly done math formulas. He must really have been concentrating, because he was completely surprised. I won't tell you what he said.

Philip jumped up, knocking the tunafish out of my hand so that pieces of it flew all over the kitchen, where it was eaten slowly by Fleetwood and speedily by Marzipan.

Then he took the pot with lumpy white sauce off the stove, where it had luckily cooled to the temperature of a warm bath, and dumped it over my head. And then he gathered his books, including the oily math paper, and left the kitchen with a few comments describing his feelings about me, which I won't bother to mention here.

I cleaned up the white sauce, rinsed my hair under the faucet, but couldn't do much with the thick gray globs of flour that stuck to the hair like head-lice. And I called Kathy Sanders to say that a sudden family emergency would keep me from going skating with her today. "That's all right," she told me kindly. "I'd rather have Heather McClarity over, anyway."

Then I had to go to the store for more food. I got tomato soup and cheddar cheese for sandwiches and checked the drug counter for poisons to put in Philip's soup, but the store only carries stuff like hydrogen peroxide and alcohol and first-aid cream. Nothing deadly.

"I had a fight with Philip," I told Nicholas, who was sitting in the kitchen when I came home.

"So what else is new?" Nicholas asked, sharing a piece of peanut brittle with me.

"He poured the dinner on my head." I leaned over so he could see the flour-lice stuck to my hair.

"Fetching, Carlotta."

"I had to go out and buy a whole new dinner with my own allowance," I said, not in the mood for jokes.

"You'll be glad to know, then, that Philip leaves tomorrow morning for a camping trip to Great Gap with his class and he won't be back until Saturday."

"He didn't tell me."

"So there'll be a few days of peace to look forward to," he said. "Can you stand it?"

"I looked at the store for poison to put in his soup," I said, taking the cans of tomato soup out of the bag, "but I couldn't find any."

"Too extreme, Lotty. Besides, Mama would be upset."

That night Philip wouldn't eat supper with us.

"I'm not hungry," he said.

"I can't stand Lotty," he insisted when my mother objected. "I won't sit at the dinner table with her."

Mother didn't argue.

"She poisoned my soup. I overheard her telling Nicholas about it."

Mother rolled her eyes. "Oh, sure, Philip," she said. But to my great surprise, Philip was allowed to eat dinner in his room and to skip the tomato soup.

When I went upstairs to bed, Philip's sleeping bag and duffle were neatly stacked in the hall and he was lying in bed, reading a comic under the covers.

"Have a good time at Great Gap," I said, standing at the door to his room. He didn't look up from *Dr. Strange*.

"I hope you do have fun," I added a little awkwardly. He did not seem to hear me.

"I'm sorry, Philip. About the tunafish, remember?"

He put his comic book down on his stomach and looked at me in an unpleasant way.

"I remember very well," he said.

"Well, good night," I said, but I guess he'd had his fill of conversation, because he didn't answer.

As soon as Mother kissed me good night and turned off my light, I started my heroism-in-the-face-of-danger dream. Only this time the victim was Philip. This is a dream I have often had. The situation changes and so does the victim—sometimes there are a great many victims—but in all cases, I am the heroine.

Even before I close my eyes, I have imagined Great Gap, where I have never been, as a high rocky trail with a summit—in fact, two summits. There's a rickety bridge between the two mountains, and it stretches dangerously over a great gap hundreds of yards deep. If a person, even an adult, were to fall between the summits, he would die, of course.

In my dream, Philip has kindly invited me to go on his class trip to Great Gap and I have consented because I don't want to hurt his feelings.

On the bus ride to the mountains, Philip's friends tell me how much Philip likes me. They say he talks about me with love and admiration to everyone in the eighth grade. He even chooses to sit next to me in the bus.

In no time at all, the bus arrives at the base of

Great Gap and we go out for lunch. Philip gives me his jacket to sit on and all of his chocolate-nut cookies because he is watching his complexion. The trip leader meets with us during lunch and discusses the dangers of this climb, mentioning particularly the rickety bridge over the Gap, and describing in detail an accident he witnessed there.

"I don't want to go," I whisper to Philip. He squeezes my hand.

"It'll be terrific fun," he says.

"I bet," I say.

I am slower than the eighth graders, and Philip, to my surprise, is perfectly happy to walk at the back of the line with me. By the time we get to the bridge across the Great Gap, everyone else has crossed except us.

I didn't dream about the hike because it was probably three hours long and boring enough if you're hiking it, much less dreaming about hiking it. But I did imagine the bridge. In fact, just as we arrived at the summit, Andy Lopez was swinging on the bridge and the instructor on the other side was purple with anger and shouting at him.

"You've probably broken the bridge for Philip and his sister," the instructor says as Andy gets off on the other side.

And he is right. I step on the bridge first, Philip behind me, and just as I feel Philip's hand on the rope railing next to mine, there is a terrible creak and the ropes on our side of the Great Gap give way so the bridge, still attached to the summit on the other side, swings wildly between the mountains and then stops. But not before Philip has been banged against the rocks and broken his leg so I have to save him. Which I do.

The instructor is lying on his stomach, his face like a ripe grape about to explode, shouting instructions down at me.

"Hold tight!" "Get Philip's hand!" "Stay calm!" "Start pulling yourself up inch by inch!"

"I am calm," I say. The instructor is not very helpful.

It is clear that I must pull myself up by the rope rail to the end of the hanging bridge, which means climbing straight up. At the top, the instructor could have pulled me over the summit if he hadn't erupted in volcanic grape before then.

I had heard that in emergencies, people occasionally have super-human strength. So, with super-human strength, I grab Philip, throw him over my shoulders, and begin climbing. At the top, which I reach without further difficulty, the instructor lifts first Philip, then me, onto the rocks where we lay side by side—me because I am so exhausted, and Philip because of his broken leg. And about this time I must have fallen asleep, because the next thing I remembered was Mother's voice asking Philip to wake me up for school, and then Philip asking Nicho to wake me up for school because he isn't speaking to me.

"In case anybody's interested," he added.

And the last I saw of Philip was when I looked out my bedroom window and he was climbing into Mr. Gleason's jeep on his way to Great Gap.

I opened the window quickly.

"'Bye," I called to him, suddenly very worried and with good reason, although I didn't know it at the moment. "Have a good time."

He didn't look at me, but he did wave in my

direction, and I felt somewhat better. But not much.

By breakfast time on Saturday morning, the day Philip was supposed to come back from his camping trip, I had almost forgotten the fight we'd had and my Great Gap bad dream when the telephone rang.

We were all sitting in the kitchen, except Sammy who sleeps late, waiting for Daddy to make French toast. I answered the telephone, and the man on the other end said in a voice I recognized immediately as trouble that he wanted to speak to my father.

"I don't understand how that could happen," my father said. "Where were your counselors?" Without waiting for an answer, he went on, "Why didn't you call right away?" And he took down directions to Great Gap and hung up.

"They can't find Philip," he said, tossing the French toast on our plates. "He disappeared last night, sometime before the end of a hike."

He put on his coat.

"I'm coming with you," Nicholas said.

"Me, too," I said.

Mother didn't say anything. Daddy put her coat around her shoulders and helped her to the car as though she'd suddenly become an invalid. Which is how I felt. Legless. In the end, we all went to Great Gap, even Sammy, who ran from the house in his jeans and unbuttoned shirt, carrying his shoes.

The trip to Great Gap went on and on and on. What was worse is that no one talked except occasionally Nicholas, who kept asking, "When will we be there?"

"I don't know," my father said harshly.

In the back seat, I cried.

"I can't help it," I said. "It's partially my fault. I had this dream."

"I don't want to hear about your stupid dream," Nicho said.

Daddy said he was going to stop the car and let Nicholas out.

"No," I said.

"Fine," Nicho said.

"Be quiet," my mother said.

Sammy picked me up and put me on the other side of him so Nicholas and I were no longer sitting together.

"Tell me about your dream later," he whispered. I guess he knew I was just about to tell him the whole thing.

My family is not terrific in emergencies, in case you haven't guessed.

Great Gap was exactly as I'd imagined it, only I didn't expect a parking lot with the yellow St. Paul's school bus sitting in the middle. The children were outside playing Frisbee and catch, leaning against the bus, drawing with chalk on the asphalt. Daddy screeched to a stop next to the bus and hopped out. When the children saw him, they stopped what they were doing and watched him walk over to one of the counselors who was soon joined by another.

"What do you think's happened?" I asked stupidly, as Nicholas was quick to point out.

Daddy beckoned to the car and Mother got out.

"Should we all come?" I asked and started to get out.

Daddy shook his head and motioned me back to the car.

"It must be bad if we're not allowed to hear it,"

I said after Mother had left. "It must be terrible."

"Dry up," Nicholas said as though he could make it happen. "Evaporate."

I could not help myself.

"I had this dream the night before Philip left," I said.

"Later, Carlotta," Sammy said, but not before Nicholas had said a few words to me that he wouldn't have dared to say with Daddy in the car.

"I feel sick," I said, and Sammy suggested I stand outside until Mother and Daddy came back. Which they did in seconds. They climbed into the car and, without a word to any of us, Daddy pulled out of the parking lot. He drove down a narrow road very slowly and onto a dirt road that led to an open grassless field. A helicopter was hovering about twenty feet above us and coming closer. Two other counselors from St. Paul's were on the field watching it.

"They've found him," Daddy said.

"Is he dead?" I asked. I was immediately sorry, but the words just spilled out.

"No," Mother said, turning around so we could all see perfectly well that she was crying. "He's hurt his arm, they think."

Again, Mother and Daddy got out and went over to stand next to the counselors. Which left Nicholas and me in the back seat, separated by Sammy.

"Don't say a word," Nicho said.

I promised myself that I would try to be quiet.

The helicopter landed with a bounce and everyone, Mother, Daddy, and the counselors, ran over. The helicopter doors opened and a man jumped out, then another leaned out the door and, by straining, I could see Philip.

"He's sitting up," I said to Nicholas.

"You promised," he said.

"But he's okay if he's sitting up."

Nicholas was hiding his eyes.

"Look," I said. By then Philip was at the helicopter door, standing in his usual way, and it was perfectly obvious to me that the only problem was with his arm.

"Shut up."

"All he did was break his arm," I said.

Nicholas looked.

"There could be head injuries," he said.

On the way home in the car, Philip told the whole story at least six times. I counted. It went like this:

He had been hiking at the back of the line with his friend, David, who is a creep—or at least he thought David was there, which goes to show you what a creep he is—when Philip's foot slipped between two rocks and he fell. Not far. Maybe five feet at the most. But far enough to break his arm when he reached out to catch himself. So there he was with a broken arm and one foot caught between the rocks. By the time he had uncaught his foot and climbed back up to the path with his broken arm, everyone had disappeared, including wonderful David. When the group, with David the creep, finally came to their senses and realized Philip was missing, he had already taken the wrong path, hoping to catch up with them. Had it not been for the helicopter pilot called in to search for him, Philip would still be lost, maybe starving, maybe dead of hunger. Who knows? The possibilities are endless.

But there he was in his own cozy car, being asked again and again by Mother and Daddy, even Sammy and Nicho, to tell the same story over and over.

"Did you just decide to go to sleep when it got dark?" Daddy asked for about the fourth time.

"He's already told you," I said.

"Jealous," Nicholas said.

"Of what?" I snapped.

"Of our hero, Carlotta," Nicho said in his least pleasant voice.

We had to go to the hospital to have Philip's arm set and then to lunch at Piago's for pizza. By the time we got home the day was gone and Philip was asleep on my lap with his broken arm on my knee in its damp plaster cast, smelling of milk of magnesia.

He was still asleep when we parked in the driveway and everyone got out and went in the back door, leaving just Philip and me in the car.

"Are you asleep?" I asked.

"Sort of," he said.

"Are you still mad at me about the other night?" I asked. He didn't answer.

I told him about my Great Gap dream anyway. And that's when we made our pact about bad dreams.

After Philip was in bed and Mother had kissed him good night a hundred and fifty times and Sammy had made him a double-thick chocolate milkshake, I came in and climbed up on his bunk.

"I'm sorry about the dream," I said.

If you liked this book,
you'll love Susan Shreve's mystery thriller

Lucy Forever and Miss Rosetree, Shrinks

When sixth graders Lucy Childs and Rosie Treeman decide to become the world-famous psychiatrists Lucy Forever and Miss Rosetree, they do it as a game. And at first it is. Their pretend practice includes a number of interesting patients, like the girl who grows black stripes on her belly because she's in love with a zebra. Yet nothing in their experience can prepare Lucy and Rosie for a little girl named Cinder, a real-life psychiatric patient with eyes full of terror and a bright red scar across her throat.

"Good characters and dialogue, a strong and unusual plot, and excellent narrative flow."
—*Bulletin of the Center for Children's Books* (starred review)

"The blend of melodrama and solid storytelling make this an entertaining thriller.... A fresh, inventive book."
—*Booklist*

Winner of the Edgar Award for Best Mystery

A BULLSEYE BOOK PUBLISHED BY ALFRED A. KNOPF, INC.

*A horse story that
"equine enthusiasts will return to again and again."***

A Summer of Horses
by Carol Fenner

Faith can't believe it! Here she was all set to have a wonderful summer at Beth Holbein's horse farm, learning to ride—and she's just discovered that horses scare her to death. She's always loved animals, but somehow she never realized before just how big and powerful and...well, *dangerous* horses are. To make matters worse, Faith's boy-crazy older sister, who doesn't even like animals, is turning out to be a good rider. It's going to be a disastrous summer if Faith doesn't learn to love horses—and quick!

FIRST TIME IN PRINT!

*Publishers Weekly

A BULLSEYE BOOK PUBLISHED BY ALFRED A. KNOPF, INC.

Betty Miles

"is solid gold!" —*Publishers Weekly*

THE SECRET LIFE OF THE UNDERWEAR CHAMP

Starring in television commercials sure isn't what it's cracked up to be discovers ten-year-old Larry Pryor. The shooting schedule conflicts with his baseball practice, and he actually has to wear makeup on film! But the biggest problem is what Larry's supposed to be modeling. They can't really expect him to go on TV in his underwear... can they?

"Yay! for a fast-reading book that's sure-fire fun."
                                                    —*School Library Journal*

"Thoroughly enjoyable, from start to finish!"
                                                    —*The Los Angeles Times*

An IRA-CBC Children's Choice
A Child Study Association Children's Book of the Year
A Georgia Children's Book Award Winner
A Mark Twain Award Winner

A BULLSEYE BOOK PUBLISHED BY ALFRED A. KNOPF, INC.